# HARRY
## and the Guinea Pig

# HARRY

Based on the character created by

# and the Guinea Pig

## Gene Zion and Margaret Bloy Graham

Written by Nancy Lambert and illustrated by Saba Joshaghani
in the styles of Gene Zion and Margaret Bloy Graham

**HARPER**

*An Imprint of HarperCollinsPublishers*

Library of Congress Control Number: 2019951150
ISBN 978-0-06-274773-0

The artist used Adobe Photoshop to create the illustrations for this book.
20 21 22 23 24 RTLO 10 9 8 7 6 5 4 3 2 1
❖
First Edition

Harry was a white dog with black spots who liked
everything about his neighborhood, except . . .
the neighbor's pet guinea pig.
One day, the guinea pig came over to play but did
not go home. Harry was *not* pleased.

The children gave the guinea pig all kinds of
new toys. They fed the guinea pig special treats.

And they gave her lots and lots of belly rubs.
No one had rubbed Harry's belly all day—not even once!

Harry didn't like the guinea pig getting *all* the attention.
Suddenly, Harry had an idea. He needed to be more like
the guinea pig.

First, he tried to look like a guinea pig. He squished his ears down and hid his tail. He twitched his nose. But nobody noticed him.

Then Harry tried to act like a guinea pig. He did tricks like the guinea pig. He sat up on his back legs and he balanced on a ball, just like she did.

But the children still didn't notice Harry.

Harry tried to play inside the guinea pig's tube.

But he was too big.

Harry watched the guinea pig run in circles around her pen. He could run around in circles, too. So Harry ran and ran and ran until he got so dizzy, he fell over.

Then Harry tried making a little nest for himself out of paper, just like the guinea pig's nest.

But the family scolded Harry for making a mess
and sent him outside.
Nothing Harry tried had worked. The guinea pig
was still getting all the attention.

Then Harry heard the children say that show-and-tell was the next day. The children *always* brought Harry. He'd do all his tricks, and everyone would forget about the guinea pig!

But on the way to school the next day, Harry discovered that someone else would be joining them.
Oh no! The guinea pig was going to show-and-tell, too!

What if the children forgot all about him?
Harry had an idea. Before it was time for show-and-
tell, he would climb into the cage with the guinea
pig. Then everyone would have to notice him.

So when no one was looking, Harry pushed
open the door to the guinea pig's cage. But
he just couldn't fit inside.

Then Harry realized he had a much BIGGER
problem. The guinea pig was gone!
"Where did the guinea pig go?" cried the children.
They searched everywhere.
Harry felt awful. He didn't like the guinea pig, but
he never thought the guinea pig would escape.

Harry knew what he had to do. He would use all his
special detective skills to find the guinea pig.
He sniffed around the empty cage until he found the
guinea pig's scent. Harry followed the scent to . . .

the art room!
But all Harry could smell was paint. Harry
squinted his eyes and spotted some tiny blue
paw prints leading out to . . .

. . . the playground!
But the rain had washed away the guinea
pig's paw prints. Even that didn't make Harry
give up.

Harry perked his ears and listened very
carefully. He thought he heard tiny squeaks,
so he followed the sounds to . . .

. . . the library!
But when Harry pushed some books off the shelf
to see if the guinea pig was hiding, there was a
*CRASH!* And he still didn't find the guinea pig.

But Harry would not give up. He sniffed again and
smelled the guinea pig. So he followed the scent out
of the library and into . . .

. . . the cafeteria!
But the cafeteria was full of too many smells.
All Harry could smell was lunch!

Then, from across the cafeteria, Harry heard a big, loud *CRUNCH!*

*Crunch! Crunch! Crunch!* There was the guinea pig!
Harry howled until the children came running.

The children clapped and cheered. "You did it, Harry! You found the guinea pig!"
And when it was time for show-and-tell, the children told everyone about the guinea pig's adventure and Harry's clever detective work.

That night, the neighbor came over to pick up
the guinea pig. The children were a little sad to
say goodbye, but they knew she would be back
to visit another day.
Harry decided it would be fine if the guinea pig
visited again. But, for now, it was good to get
back to his old tricks.